A Grandpa Like Yours

by Andria Warmflash Rosenbaum

illustrated by Barb Björnson

KAR-BEN
PUBLISHING

GLOSSARY

Bubbe – grandma (Yiddish)

Challah – Sabbath bread

Horah – Israeli folkdance

Kugel – noodle pudding

Menorah – candelabraum used on Hanukkah

Matzah – unleavened bread eaten on Passover

Mitzvah – good deed

Purim – holiday commemorating Queen
      Esther's rescue of the Jews

Saba – grandpa (Hebrew)

Savta – grandma (Hebrew)

Seder – ritual meal at Passover

Shofar – ram's horn blown on High Holidays

Shul – synagogue

Tallit – prayer shawl

Tu B'Shevat – birthday of the trees

Zayde – grandpa (Yiddish)

Text copyright © 2006 by Andrea Warmflash Rosenbaum
Illustrations copyright © 2006 by Barb Björnson

Kar-Ben Publishing
A division of Lerner Publishing Group, Inc.
241 First Avenue North
Minneapolis, MN 55401 U.S.A.
1-800-4-KARBEN

Website address: www.karben.com

Library of Congress Cataloging-in-Publication Data

Rosenbaum, Andria Warmflash, 1958–
   A grandma like yours ; A grandpa like yours / by Andria Warmflash Rosenbaum
: illustrations by Barb Björnson.
     p. cm.
   Titles from separate title pages; works issued back-to-back and inverted.
  Summary: Two rhyming stories of wonderful Jewish grandmothers and grandfathers.
   ISBN-13: 978–1–58013–167–4 (lib. bdg. : alk. paper)
   ISBN-10: 1–58013–167–0 (lib. bdg. : alk. paper)
   1. Upside-down books—Specimens. [1. Grandmothers—Fiction. 2. Grandfathers—Fiction. 3. Jews—Fiction. 4. Stories in rhyme. 5. Upside-down books. 6. Toy and movable books.] I. Björnson, Barbara, 1952– ill. II. Rosenbaum, Andria Warmflash, 1958– Grandpa like yours. III. Title. IV. Title : Grandpa like yours.
PZ8.3.R72245Gra 2006
[E]—dc22   2005004480

Manufactured in Hong Kong
3 – PN – 1/1/15

051521.7K2/B0632

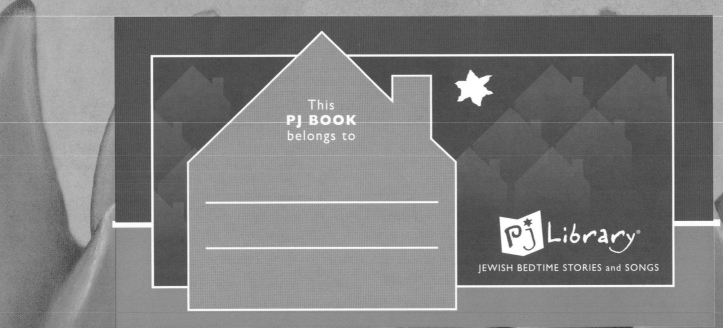

This
PJ BOOK
belongs to

PJ Library®

JEWISH BEDTIME STORIES and SONGS

A *zayde*, a **saba**
No two are the same
Each **GRANDPA** is special
Whatever his name.

Do **sabas of llamas** blow shofar each year

So ears young and
old hear the call
loud and clear?

But what about **quail sabas** . . .

. . . snail sabas, too?

Can they mix up a kugel
that's tasty to chew?

Do zebras have **ZAYDES** who love to parade

In Israel's honor with banners they made?

Do **porcupine papas** help with matzah-making

By counting the minutes
that it has been baking?

Do **zaydes of sheep** share their tallit in shul

When grandlambs' teeth chatter
because it's too cool?

Do **grandpas of groundhogs** plant Tu B'Shevat trees

Outside in the sun in dirt up to their knees?

A grandpa, a zayde, a saba, a pop
Your grandpa is certain
to come out on top.

You may call her bubbe or
savta or nanny

Whatever you call her,
she's your favorite granny.

For 23 cousins all equally dear?

Do grandmother bunnies **make seders each year**

Bringing soup to the sick
with a rose on the tray?

Does a grandma giraffe do a mitzvah a day

Delivering baskets of
yummy surprises?

Can beau-wowing bubbes wear Purim disguises

Preparing to light her silver menorah?

Does a kangaroo savta like dancing the horah

Then lace up their
sneakers to have
a quick catch?

Do chimpanzee nanas bake challah from scratch

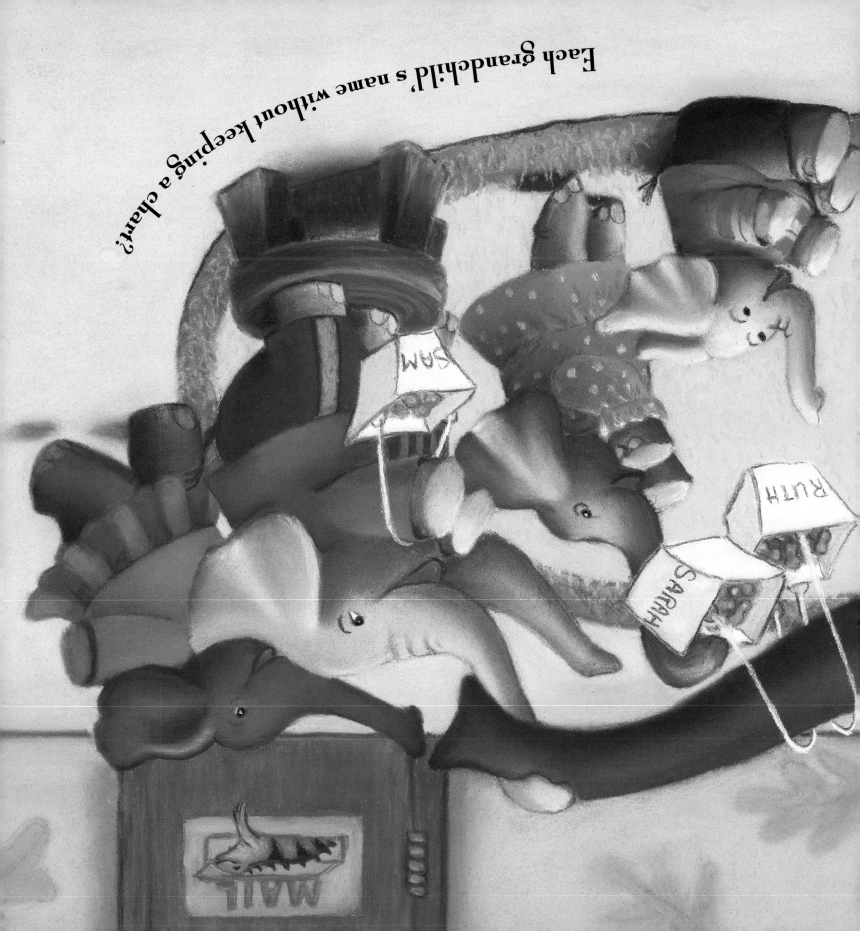

Each grandchild's name without keeping a chart?

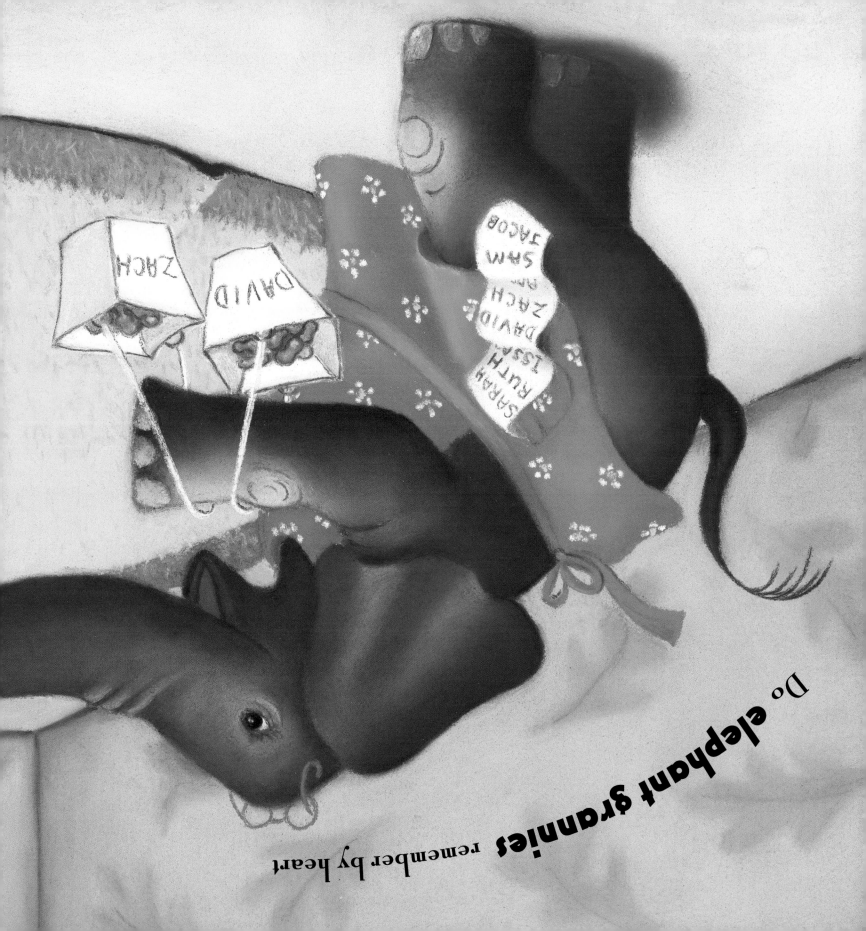

Do elephant grannies remember by heart?

A *bubbe*, a **savta**

No two are the same

Each **GRANDMA** is special

Whatever her name.

For Savta and Saba Warmflash
and
Bubbe and Zayde Rosenbaum,
each a grandchild's wish!
— A.W.R

To Matta, a very loving Amma and dear friend,
and
Mabel who has love in her heart for all of us.
— B.K.B.

A Grandma Like Yours

by Andria Warmflash Rosenbaum

illustrated by Barb Bjornson

KAR-BEN
PUBLISHING